The Bigger Fish

Two Girls, One Guy,
Some Choices

Magdel Roets
Writer of Christian Fiction

PO Box 221974 Anchorage, Alaska 99522-1974
books@publicationconsultants.com—www.publicationconsultants.com

ISBN 978-1-59433-646-1
eISBN 978-1-59433-647-8
Library of Congress Catalog Card Number: 2016945307

Copyright 2016 Magdel Roets
—First Edition—

All rights reserved, including the right of
reproduction in any form, or by any mechanical
or electronic means including photocopying or
recording, or by any information storage or
retrieval system, in whole or in part in any
form, and in any case not without the
written permission of the author and publisher.

Manufactured in the United States of America.

Contents

Chapter 1	A Visit to an Art Gallery	5
Chapter 2	Having too much Fun	13
Chapter 3	Small Fish Trouble	19
Chapter 4	Bigger Trouble	25
Chapter 5	Going Down	31
Chapter 6	Change	43
Chapter 7	The Trap	55
Chapter 8	Liza	63
Chapter 9	Tommy	75
Chapter 10	Caught	83

Chapter 1

A Visit to an Art Gallery

The students move from one painting to the next, studying everyone carefully according to their limited knowledge and understanding of the fine arts. Liza elbows her friend and roommate in the ribs and points out a man standing on the other side of the hall:

"Oooooh, look at that guy. Isn't he a catch!" Annoyed, her concentration broken, Joni frowns at Liza and says, scowling: "For goodness sakes, Liza, we're not here to find guys. We're here to learn. You can go guy-hunting afterward."

"How will I find him, if I don't make a move now?"

"Who says he'd be interested? He looks pretty much interested in art, not girls if you ask me."

"Well, I'm not asking you. You're such a spoilsport. I can feel this guy is going to change my life, I just know it. I'm going to move over and ..."

"Can you see what I'm talking about, students?" The lecturer leading the tour points out a topic of interest that was discussed in class the previous day. "See how the artist used his own technique to blend into the style of the Impressionists?" Joni grabs Liza by the arm and drags her along while the lecturer continues to the next hall where the work of Francine Hammond was being displayed.

"Come, Liza, I'm not going to fill you in on what Me. Paintbrush says today. You're going to hear all of it yourself." Rolling her big, grey eyes, Liza stops sketching and moves along with the group, her curly blond ponytails swinging over her ears.

"Listen carefully now, students. The work of this artist just might appear in question form in the next test. Francine Hammond is one of our finest South-African artists of this decade." Liza puts her sketchpad under her arm and starts making notes of the comments of the lecturer.

Back in their apartment Liza opens her sketchpad and sits down to finish her sketch while she can still remember the features of the man in the gallery. Joni joins her at the kitchen table with steaming cups of hot chocolate. Liza has a remarkable talent to lay down a recognizable portrait in a matter of minutes. At this moment, Joni watches her finalizing the detail of a face she has seen only for a few minutes. The shadow around the eyes emphasizing the intense concentration with which he studied the painting on the wall in front of him, the shine of the hair as the light caught it on one side, the half-smile on the lips; the finished sketch, a perfect image of the face of a man she might never see again.

Joni studies the sketch and thought the same as Liza: quite a catch. A face full of character, and very, very attractive. Too attractive. Right now she had to focus on her studies. She cannot afford to be distracted by men, however good-looking. But, oh, those deep-dark brown eyes. They could probably melt steal. To Liza she said: "Amazing, Liza. I will never understand how you do it. To sketch a face so accurately in such a short time."

"Practice makes perfect. You've seen how I carry my sketchbook everywhere I go. I've sketched everything I see since I could hold a pencil."

"Still. Even if I try it, I'll never be as good as you. It's a God-given talent".

"Glad you like it," she said humbly and closed the book to prevent more praises that embarrassed her. She rinsed her cup and put it away. *God-given talent*, Liza thought. When did Joni become religious?

"I'm going to go over my notes and then I'm going to take a long, warm bath and off to bed."

"Right. I still have to finish my assignment before I can go to bed."

****

Quintin Trout pulls his fingers through his thick, dark brown hair. What shall I write about these artists whose work I saw today? He decided to research their backgrounds before starting his article for "Arts and Sculptures Monthly". As a start-up artist he had to write freelance reviews for magazines to keep bread on the table for him and his stepbrother, Tommy, who stayed with him while in college. On the Google screen, he typed in the name of one artist. Jim Atkins. Wikipedia has a lot on Jim Atkins, but Quintin also checked out other sites and pages, like Facebook, as well as the artist's personal website.

He made notes as far as he went, but when he started to write his article, he merely worked the information he gathered into his own opinion of Jim Atkin's work. He did the same for the other artists, Andrea Jones, Lizbeth Bachman, Vic Thomson. They all have a lot in common and his article flowed nicely from his fingers onto the computer screen.

When he came to Francine Hammond, he realized her history was a little different from the others. Other artists usually profess a deep love for the arts from an early age, and starting to sketch and taking lessons from the time they could hold a pencil or brush. Francine discovered her interest after she had already left school and was backpacking through Europe in search of her "destiny." After two years in Europe, Francine went back, studied art, acquired her Master's Degree, a Teachers Diploma and opened her own art school in Johannesburg, before going, back to Cape Town where she currently runs her late father's company, and, with her husband, raised two children, of whom at least one, her son Robert Crompton, is fast becoming a recognized artist in his own right.

What made Francine Hammond more noticeable, was that her art has a unique style created by techniques she developed while teaching art to her students. All her paintings had a character of its own, told a tale no one has ever told before. Writing about her, was a pleasure more than a chore for Quintin, adding his own interpretation of the work.

Having proofread his article twice, Quintin pressed the "send" button and logged out. It was almost midnight and time to catch some sleep so that he can rise early to finish a painting or two that had been nagging him for weeks. Five more paintings, and he'd be ready to approach an art gallery to consider exhibiting his work. Maybe someone will soon review his work. Won't that be nice!

****

Receiving her test paper from the lecturer, Joni couldn't help but smiling. An A symbol, as usual. She studied hard and did her utmost to do good, acquire as much knowledge as she possibly could. Not as talented as most students, she made up for it with good academic grades. Knowing she might not become the world's greatest painter, she might end up a curator or even a lecturer. She'd be happy either way, as long as she can work with art and artists for as long as she can keep a career on track.

"C-plus," Liza sulked next to Joni as soon as they walked out into the sunshine. "I was like hoping for a B. Next time I'll show old Missus Paintbrush I can do it."

"She knows you can do it, but she also knows you get easily distracted. And when you're distracted, you don't study effectively. But she also knows you are the most talented of all the students on campus." Joni lay a hand on her shoulder for a little encouragement.

"Thank you. It makes me feel like a whole lot better. Still, I'd like to do better in my theoretical tests. But, what the heck. It's over and it's like time to party. Where are we hanging out tonight?"

"You go on and party. I still have one more test to write before the series are over."

"Come on! It's just one night. Your test is in two days. You'll still cut it if you take a break tonight. It's like if I'm the most talented, you're the cleverest. Don't be such a bore. Come tonight and study tomorrow night."

"Okay, okay. But I won't stay till midnight. I'll have a couple of drinks, dance a little and then I'm outa there."

"Whatever. Let's go see what we'll wear."

"First we'll eat. And no snorting tonight. If you go snorting, I'm outa there real quick."

Liza grabbed Joni by the arm and said: "Well let's get going then. I'm starving." She led the way to the student cafeteria and Joni, not in the mood to prepare a meal at home, tagged along willingly. But the moment they enter the cafeteria, she realized it was a mistake.

"Hi, Liza, hi Joni," said Penny, one of the junky former friends of Liza, that Joni managed to get Liza away from. She was always among a crowd of junkies and high most of the time.

"Wanna join us?" Penny waves Liza over. "Haven't seen you in weeks. Everything cool?"

"Yeah, cool." Liza waved a hand at Penny, but passed her table to go and sit with Joni at a table in the corner farthest away from Penny's crowd. Nevertheless, Joni tried to eavesdrop on Penny's conversation with her friends, knowing they would be going to some club. She heard them talking about The Peacock and decided she and Liza would choose any other club, but The Peacock.

"I feel like going to The Goose and Gander tonight. How about it?" Thinking for a moment, Liza replied:

"Yea, Okay. Funny that a club with a name that sucks can be so cool. Yeah. Goose and Gander it is."

Dressed in short skirts, skintight tops, their hair done in a trendy curly style, they left their second story apartment in the building that housed ten apartments, at eight that night, ready for the party at the club two blocks away.

Chapter 2

Having too much Fun

Gyrating to the rhythm of earsplitting music in a smoke-filled room, the girls enjoyed the evening away from books and studying, after a semester of hard work and little fun. To relax, Joni had a shooter and Liza had three. Joni puffed a joint with a nice boy, but Liza was looking for something stronger when she feels a tap on her shoulder. Penny standing behind her said: "It's like nice to see ya, Lizzy. Whatta ya up to girl?"

"Hav'n fun and look'n for more. You?"

"You know me, I'm always hav'n fun." She turned to the boy at her side and giggled. "And this dude has pockets full of fun, haven't you, Tommy baby?"

"You dig. Pockets full," he boasts, slapping his pants pockets, chuckling foolishly.

"Want some?"

"Aw, man. I'm sorta broke. If I'd known you'd be here, I'd make a plan."

"We went to The Peacock first, but there's a new bouncer. Strict rules, ya know. Bet he's 'n undercover cop or som'tn."

"Undercover cop, yeah," repeats the boy. He was obviously not a man of many words, except when he sees a good deal thrown at him. As soon as Penny turned her back on them, he made his move: "Look, Liza, I know it's tough to be wanting something badly and not having the cash to pay for it. But I got the stuff and you got a gorgeous body. Seeing it's a first fix, I can help you out and you pay me with ... you know, something else."

"You're disgusting. Aren't you and Penny an item?"

"Don't make me laugh. Penny is not a girl you hook up with for longer than one night. I know her. She's a party animal. She'll go on through the night and give me what I want in the early hours. But I need it now. How about it? I give to you and you give to me. And what I give, is good stuff. Really, really good stuff. What ya say? We go upstairs briefly?" Liza was considering the possibilities when Penny rejoined them. At this very moment Joni found them, shooting Liza a killing look.

"Come on, Liza, time to go."

"It's like the fun is just starting, Joni. Light'n up."

"No, we need to go. It's late."

"You go, then. I'm not ready to turn in yet, Grandma." This sent Penny and the boy almost to the floor, laughing.

"You're stoned already. Come on. Let's go."

"And I told you, Grandma, I'm not go'n." Turning her back on Joni, Liza grabbed Penny and the boy by their arms and gyrated in the opposite direction. Joni, undecided at first, went to the ladies-room, then went looking for Liza again, but did not see her anywhere.

Letting her eyes wander through the smoky room, she thought she saw a familiar face, but then it was gone again. Where did she see those curly brown hair and smoldering brown eyes? The moment of contact was so brief, she soon convinced herself it was her imagination, yet, the thrill of the moment lingered. Having those eyes looking so intently into hers, sent shockwaves through her whole body. Then he looked away again and she doubted what she saw. But how could it not be real? It was so intense, it must have been real. No longer in a hurry to leave, she decided to look for Liza one more time. Then maybe she would see Brown-eyes again. No such luck, she saw neither anywhere.

Reluctantly she turned around to head home, and there he was. Right in front of her, she almost bumped into him. He grabbed her arm to keep her from losing her balance, staring one more time intently into her eyes, then turned away quickly, mumbling an excuse and headed for the staircase that lead to the upper rooms on top of the club. Frozen in place for a moment, Joni just stood there. Couldn't think, couldn't move. When she finally did move, it was with badly coordinated jerks that made her look like the puppet of an unexperienced puppeteer.

How she reached home, she could not remember. All she was sure of, was the touch of Brown-eyes' hand on her arm. Reliving the moment his hand touched her skin, her legs turned to Jell-O.

Meanwhile at the club Quintin went in search of his little stepbrother, convinced he was up to no good, as usual. He was right. Tommy was undressing the girl with the blond curly hair in a dark corner when Quintin grabbed him by the collar of his shirt and dragged him away. Turning back, he saw the embarrassment on the girl's face as she buttoned up her blouse.

"Hurry, cover yourself and I'll take you home." She shook her head, looking at him with big, unnaturally bright, grey eyes. He took her arm, gently but firmly and led her down the stairs, dragging his protesting stepbrother by the neck with his other hand.

"Where do you live?" Liza mumbled the address of her student apartment as he bundled them both into his car. Just a couple of blocks down the road, he stopped and let Liza out, watching as she disappeared into the building. He waited until he saw a light coming on in a second story window, then drove off with Tommy sulking in the back seat.

Before he went to bed, Quintin checked on Tommy snoring away loudly. His thoughts kept on returning to the girl at the club. Those kind-looking, almond-colored eyes, the curly dark hair in a style that accentuated the curve of her strong and beautiful jawline. It seemed she was looking for someone, but seemed bewildered when she saw him. Why would that be? Did she know him? And knowing him, why that strange look in her eyes as if she recognized him, but not wanting to talk to him?

Maybe he was just tired. Maybe it was all just his imagination. Besides, why worry about a girl who hangs out in a club like that. She was probably looking for someone who could give her a fix. With this, he tried, unsuccessfully to ban the thoughts of the girl from his mind. After two mugs of hot chocolate, reading seventeen Psalms from his Bible and hours of staring at the ceiling but seeing the girl's face, he finally fell asleep.

****

Partly it was fury that kept Joni awake. How could Liza treat her like that. Calling her 'grandma', imagine. If she was not stoned, she would have heard it tonight, or rather this morning as it was past midnight. She heard Liza coming in, but pretended to be asleep. But tonight, Liza is going to listen to a few things she might not like to hear. Enough is enough. Joni warned her and this is it: tomorrow Joni is going to look for another apartment. She will not share her living space with a junky, even if it only happens sporadically. It will not end there. It always leads to addiction and goes from bad to worse.

Just as Joni's anger flared up again, the image of Mr. Brown-eyes appeared in her head. Again. What was a guy who had so much appreciation for art, doing in a place like that? This question made her feel like a hypocrite. What was she doing in a place like that? She shivered at the thought of him touching her. What would it be like if he held her in his arms? That was a thought she could easily fall asleep with.

When the alarm went off in the morning, Joni felt as if she had just fallen asleep. After two cups of strong, sweet instant coffee, she took a shower and made ready for class. Her eyes caught the overfull trashcan. Ugh, my turn to empty the thing. She grabbed the inside can from the peddle bin and emptied it in the big container outside. As she turned, her eyes caught a small piece of paper stuck on the inside of the can. She looked into the big container and saw a number of small pieces, all marked with pencil.

Curious now, Joni took a few pieces and tried to put them together on the kitchen table, those that were not too badly soiled. It would be impossible to put together the whole sketch, but there were enough pieces for Joni to see it was a sketch of a face, the handsome face of Mr, Brown-eyes. Why on earth would Liza tear up such a good sketch? And this one in particular? Did she see him at the club last night? Did he say something to her? Realizing it was getting late, she left the half-finished sketch puzzle on the kitchen table, grabbed her bag and left for class.

Chapter 3

Small Fish Trouble

On the second floor of the library, where all the books on Geology were kept, Tommy was waiting in a booth hidden away behind large shelves filled with thick, dusty books. His face lid up when he saw the cute blond girl approaching him. Liza sat down next to him and smiled.

"You got something for me?"

"A kiss first, and then business." She draped her arms around him and kissed him intimately. The kiss lasted several minutes accompanied by some groping before Liza broke away gulping for air. Tommy wanted more of that, but Liza was unwilling to give too much too soon.

"Your turn, Baby. Let's see the stuff." He took a small packet from the inner pocket of his denim jacket and handed it to her. She hid the packet in her bra and in return, handed him a handful of Dollar notes. Making out some more, Liza finally pulled away and told him it was time for the next class. As she walked away, he called her back: "Liza." She turned, waved and said: "See ya."

"Liza, wait. Can I see you again?"

"Of course. I'll need more of this stuff soon enough."

"No, I mean, can I take you out?"

"Like in a date?"

"Yeah. Like a date." She smiled and nodded: "Sure. Call me." I'm not good enough for big brother Brown-eyes, so Tommy will have to do, she thought. And he's cute enough. Walking away from Tommy at a fast pace, she thought of his brother; the one who dragged them away from the club. Those eyes, shoulders, that steady, purposeful walk, everything about him just turned her on. Sighing, she decided he was just so far above her type. She'd never be in his league.

When she got home Joni was already there. She left in such a hurry that morning, there was time to have a quick drink of juice and nothing more. Seeing the "puzzle" of the torn-up drawing neatly lain out on the table was a shock to her. She'd hoped to get home early and destroy it properly before Joni got home, but her room mate surprised her. And now it was Q & A-time. Joni immediately started shooting questions at her.

"Why, Liza? Why did you tear up this sketch? It was one of the best?"

"No, it wasn't. I just didn't like it."

"Oh, no. You're not fooling me. There's something else behind it, isn't there?"

"What's this? Twenty questions? What is it to you what I do with my sketches? I can tear them all up and it's none of your business."

"Sorry for being alive. I was just showing some interest."

"Well thanks a lot. But it really is nothing." Joni could see in Liza's eyes there is a lot more to it.

"Come on, Roomy, what's bothering you. You know you can trust me. Out with it." Liza started telling the whole story about Tommy and his big brother, who happened to be Mr. Brown-eyes, as they both began to call him. That stunning guy from the gallery. Joni's heart leapt at the news that he was not visiting the club, but rescuing his brother from it. And Liza too. What a hero!

"...and it's like I've stopped dreaming about a guy like that ..." Joni heard her flat-mate saying. "Just not in his league, y'know."

"Baloney. There's no such thing as a league. All people have the same value."

"Not me. I'm damaged goods. Have been since I was six. Stepdad made sure of that." Speechless, Joni just stared at her. When she found her voice again, she said: "I hate stepdads. They ruin everything."

"You too?" Liza asked in disbelief.

"Yeah. Me too." She nodded, staring at the pattern on the tablecloth. "Me too. And how many other girls?"

"You never can tell."

"No, you can't. But we all end up with some weird kind of behavior".

"Yeah. Like eating disorders, drug abuse, whoring, cutting. My sister started stealing things. She's doing time."

"Flip, Liza, I'm so sorry." She added a few foul words, then continued: "But it's not us. We're not the guilty ones. It's them."

"Yeah. And they get away with it."

"Not always. My stepdad is doing time right now. Ten years, seven to go. My Mom finally believed us and did something about it."

"Not my Mom. She took his side. Told me I asked for it. That's why I chose this college. The farthest one from home where I was accepted. She screamed and pleaded for me to take the closest one so I can stay at home. Just packed my bags, got on the bus and here I am. Never been back. Never been happier."

"Good for you. See, you can make good choices. Keep it up, girl. Don't let his sin define you. You're your own person."

"Joni, you're such a good friend. Almost like a sister. Better than a sister. Now let's have coffee and a bite. I'm starving."

****

Quintin stood back to looked at his painting. Finished. Wiping his brushes on a cloth, he looked closely to see if he can find something he would like to change. Nope, this painting went very well. Every brush stroke was perfectly placed in the exact color to get the effect he wanted. Looks like you're getting it. Stick with this theme, and you might see success someday, he told himself. Tomorrow he will take pictures and then visit the gallery he had been in contact with about a possible exhibition.

He took his brushes and gave them a good rinsing in white-spirits before he washed them with soap and water.

He switched off the light but did not close the door. With the window and the door both open, the smell of paint and white-spirits would not build up. Satisfied with the day's work, he washed his hands and went to the kitchen to make himself a cup of coffee. Tommy entered and pored himself a cup too, then sat down at the table.

"Hi, Quint, can we go somewhere tonight. I've been a good boy for three months now? Whadaya say. Let's go somewhere. Anywhere. And you can hold my hand all night long. As long as I get out of here a bit."

"Not tonight, Tommy. I have a church meeting. But tomorrow night I'm free. Let's do something tomorrow. There are ball games on, or we can go to the movies."

"Movies? With you? Man, come on. What if my buddies see us? They'll think I've gone queer. No way. See if you can get tickets for one of the ball games. That'll be cool."

"Right. I agree. Ball game it'll be. And afterward we can grab a pizza or two."

"And beer," Tommy said, grinning. Quintin frowned at him: "Watch it. Don't push your luck. It's a long way before I'll let you get near alcohol. Ginger is the closest you'll get to beer as long as you're with me. You need to dry out completely and it's not going to be quick. I'm proud of you so far. So, don't blow it now."

"Okay, okay, I'm getting it. I'll have a bubblegum milkshake instead." Quintin just shook his head and finished his coffee.

"Listen, I won't be long, but get yourself something to eat. Here. Be sure to be here when I get back." He handed him some cash and headed for the door.

"Sure. Early night for me. I might be fast asleep by then."

"Finish your assignments first," he replied and left.

Chapter 4

Bigger Trouble

The noise of something falling, woke Quintin out of a deep sleep. It also sounded like wood breaking and the sound came from the room where his paintings were. What? He thought, burglars? Quietly he got out of bed and took his baseball bat in his hand, hoping the burglars were not armed with firearms. He stopped in his tracks when he heard giggling. It sounded like a girl. What the heck? He switched on the lights and found the source of the noise and giggling on the floor of his studio. Legs twisted together, groping and kissing were Tommy and a girl on top of his newest painting. The one he had finished earlier that day. He took a swing at Tommy's head with the bat, but making sure to miss.

"What do you think you're doing. Get up, the two of you." They tried but failed, all the while giggling. Quintin noticed it was the same girl from the club when he dragged them both home. When they were finally on their feet, clothes blotched with wet paint, he picked up his painting, the one he was particularly proud of. Totally ruined. Besides that, the stretching frame was broken in two places. That must have been the breaking sound he had heard.

As he turned, he noticed two small packets on the floor. Tommy saw what he was looking at, and bent to grab it, but Quintin beat him to it. He grabbed them up before Tommy could reach down. Tommy tried to get the packets away from him, overbalanced, grabbed at the nearest thing to keep him from falling. The nearest thing, were a stack of finished paintings that came crashing down with Tommy. The girl stood watching wide eyed, but started giggling again.

"Shut up, you little tart," yelled Quintin. "Get your purse and come along." He grabbed Tommy by the collar, grabbed his car keys and bundled them both in his car, just like the night at the club. It was a good thing that the late night chill caused him to go to bed in a tracksuit. No time to waste getting dressed. Remembering the girl's address, he drove her there and pulled away as soon as he saw the second story light go on. By the time they reached the highway, Tommy was snoring. He must have been stoned properly.

Quintin took his cell phone from his pocket and speed dialed a number.

"Yea, Quint, what's up. Is it Tommy?"

"Yea. Can I bring him in? Now?"

"Of course. I told you any time he screws up you bring him to me."

"Thanks, man. See you in a couple of hours. We're on our way already."

"Sure. Be waiting. Safe driving."

****

The halfway house is open twenty-four hours a day with someone always on duty to take in new-comers. Collin was always available to help with the process. He never minded being woken up for emergencies like that. They met each other at a summer camp for boys, many years ago. Collin learned in those days about Tommy, the naughty little stepbrother. They kept in contact and Collin kept track of Tommy's behavior getting worse.

When Quintin stopped in front of the halfway house, Collin was waiting. He helped getting Tommy out of the car and into the house, where he was taken to a room smaller than a prison cell. He was stripped of his belt and everything else that might be potentially dangerous. The two male nurses tending to him also got him out of his clothes and into a boxer trunk and put him to bed after recording his vitals on a chart.

Collin promised to be there when the rehab clinic opened in the morning. He would personally handle Tommy's admission. After a brief exchange between the two men, Quintin left and went to the hotel that Collin recommended. He was too tired to drive all the way back home. Though he was in a hurry to assess the damage to his paintings, he realized the danger of driving in the condition he was in. In the morning he would first call Ted Trout, Tommy's father - his stepfather - and then take on the long drive home.

****

"Morning, Quintin. What can I do for you?"
"Morning Ted. I'm calling from The Haven Rehabilitation Centre."

"Tommy?"

"Yea. Brought him in last night. Just been transferred from the halfway house. Thought I'd let you know myself."

"Is he in bad shape?"

"Not really. He was doing quite well and confident he'd make it on his own. I was keeping a strict eye on him. You know. Didn't let him go anywhere without me, and he complied."

"So, what happened?"

"He wanted to go out last night, but I had a church meeting, so I promised him a ball game tonight. I got home later than usual. I went straight to bed instead of checking in on him. He came in, in the early hours, stoned, brought a stoned girl along. So, I bundled him in the car and drove straight to the halfway house." He did not mention his suspicion that Tommy was not only a user, but also a supplier.

"Didn't think he had it in him to do it outside the rehab. That boy is just too weak. Never could do anything right."

"Whatever. I'm not going to argue about it, Ted. You just never believed in him."

"Right. We have argued this thing to the bone. So, don't you lay this on me. If he wanted to make something of his life, he would have. He's just a useless human being. An oxygen thief is what he is."

"He is your son."

"Don't remind me. Anyway, thanks for calling. I'll arrange payments with administration. Hope they keep him a year."

"Doubt it. Listen, I got to go. I'll call in a week and let you know what's happening."

"Don't bother. I don't want to know."

"Right. I'll stay in touch anyway." He killed the phone and drove off.

During the five hour drive Quintin's thoughts kept returning to the events of the previous night. Was he too harsh with Tommy, dumping him in rehab? How else would he get clean? But did he react out of fury because of the damage to his paintings, or was it really the best thing he could do? For Tommy? Why did he always doubt himself where Tommy is concerned?

Then his thoughts returned to the girl. He was hoping she had learned her lesson the first time, but she was probably hooked and will go from bad to worse. If she is not stopped. He wondered if she had someone to take care of her. Get her into some sort of dry-out place. If only he could help them all. *God, what can I do. Is there anything I could do, should do?* He'd burn every club where drugs are sold, if it were possible.

The club. The girl. He tried in vain to rid his thoughts of the other girl. The one with the coppery dark hair and enquiring look in her eyes. Will he ever see her again? Where might she be? What might she be doing? Remembering her eyes, her hair, the light reflecting from her cheek and chin. He draw a deep breath to make his heart beating normal. Whenever he thought of her, his heart would jump and race at an uneven pace. *Lord, how crazy is this? How can I feel this way about a girl I don't even know?* But those eyes. They looked so deep into his soul as if they knew each other.

The Bigger Fish

****

It was almost four when he reached his apartment. He had a quick shower and shave and went to the administration building of the university to inform them that Tommy Trout would not be attending classes for at least six months. Back at his apartment he went straight to his little studio to assess the damage. The last painting, the one he finished the previous day was beyond repair. The wet paint was smudged and smeared over the full width of the canvas. Where the stretching frame had broken, the sharp ends of the wood stuck through the canvas in more than one place.

The same happened to two other paintings, those Tommy knocked over when he lost his balance trying to grab the sachet with meth from him. But at least the paint on them was dry. The second painting with broken frame did not seem to be so bad. At least the wood did not tear the canvas, just bent it. The other one was pierced, but the tear might be hidden in the framing process. It was the wet painting that was totally ruined. He'd have to scrape off the paint, cut the canvas smaller, stretch it onto a new frame and perhaps he can at least use the canvas to make another painting, starting from scratch.

Chapter 5

Going Down

Liza could not understand why Tommy did not answer his cell phone. She called several times getting voice mail. He never called back. Did Big Brother Brown-eyes forbid him to have contact with her? Did Big Brother lock him up? She smirked at the absurdity of the thought. Well, if it were over between Tommy and her, she would have to find another supplier. Penny was her only hope to get the good stuff from. Penny would know someone.

****

Joni noticed a change in her roommate. A change that spelled nothing good. Liza was withdrawn, even lethargic sometimes, other times the total opposite. Her grades went from C-plus to D. Her sketches and paintings were still good, but lacked that something special that used to make them unique and exceptional, some even weird. As if that was not enough, Liza lost her healthy appetite. Her skin turned a sickly greyish pallor. Joni made these observations over a period of months. Little by little, Liza changed and Joni, being busy with her studies, noticed when these changes became so obvious that she could no longer miss them. Neither miss nor ignore them.

Liza sat at the kitchen counter, making patterns in her cereal with the spoon, her chin resting on one hand. She dropped the spoon, took a sip of juice, then continued the pattern-drawing in the cereal. Joni, watching her, gently poked her on the hand with a forefinger.

"Roomy, what's the matter with you? You're just not yourself anymore." She just shrugged, finished her juice and got up to leave. Joni grabbed her arm, saying:

"Liza, I'm talking to you. What's with you? You just sit around lately doing nothing or going out at night, coming back before dawn and sleep through the day. Your grades are down coz you don't attend half the classes, you look terrible, skinny as a broomstick. I want to know why." Liza pulled up her sleeve. Joni, gasping exclaimed: "Liza, no, no! Why, how long?" Liza slumped down on the breakfast stool.

"I'm hooked, Joni. Need a fix often."

"That's expensive stuff. Where do you get the money?"

"Where do you think?"

"You mean ... Liza, no, you can't do this to yourself. You're self-destructing. Don't you realize where you'll end up? You're so talented and you're destroying all of it. If I can get hold of that Tommy character I'll tear him apart."

"I'm not getting it from him. He's gone. Big Brother put him in rehab, at least that's the rumor that's going around."

"Why don't you book yourself in?"

"I won't survive withdrawal. They say it's as dangerous as OD. Few people survive it."

"That's baloney and you know it. I'm going to call Student Health Support right now and I'll take you there. They will know what to do, where to send you."

"No, Joni. Don't waste your time on me. It's too late." She looked Joni in the eyes, then quickly looked away. Joni didn't like what she saw: emptiness. Why didn't she realize sooner how serious this has become, Joni thought. She saw Liza deteriorating before her eyes. This conversation should have taken place months ago. Joni felt her insides tie into a knot. How can she stop this? What should she do?

"You better go now. You'll be late for your class."

"I'm not going to class, I'm not leaving you like this."

"I'm okay, really."

"Then come with me to class."

"I'm okay, Joni, really," she repeated. Joni folded her arms over her chest and moved her head from side to side.

"Nope, you come with me, or I stay."

"Alright. Let's go then." She grabbed her bag, sulking.

"Now smile," Joni said. Liza smiled, but only with her mouth. Her eyes had an empty stare as if there were nothing to focus on, just like before. At least she's moving and getting out of the apartment, Joni thought. It might help.

****

The Bigger Fish

Quintin drove home from the gallery. His exhibition seemed to be a success. As he passed the building where he dropped Tommy's girl, he thought about her again. He had been meaning to go and see if she was doing alright, but the exhibition kept him busy and he kept putting it off. On impulse he parked and decided now was as good a time as any. He got out of his car and took the stairs to the second floor.

Working out which apartment had to be hers from the position he saw the light went on both times he dropped her off, he knocked on the door, not really expecting someone to be at home at this hour of the day. To his surprise the door did open, but it was not the blond girl who stood before him.

"Hi," shock and surprise all over Joni's face when she recognized him.

"Hi, err, sorry. I must be at the wrong place. I was looking for a girl with blond hair, ... err, ..." He felt silly, not knowing the name of the person he was looking for.

"Hi," Joni said again. "Liza? You're looking for Liza? I'm Joni, her roomy."

"Hi, Joni." Nice name, he thought, and his heart almost stopped. It suits her. "I'm Quintin. Do you know where Liza is?"

"Forgive my manners. Please come in." She stood aside and Quintin followed her inside and took the seat she offered.

"Why are you looking for Liza? She's not here right now."

"I just wanted to check up on her. She dated my brother and he is out of town for a while."

"Liza told me he is in rehab. Is that true?"

"Well, yes. And he will be for a while. What else has she told you?"

"Look, I'm going to be honest with you. Liza told me he supplied her with drugs. Since Tommy is gone, Liza found another supplier and she went on to more serious stuff. I'm worried about her. She's in bad shape and I don't even know where she is right now." Having said that, Joni could bite off her tongue for spilling the beans in front of this total stranger.

"What do you mean? When was the last time you saw her?"

"We went to classes together this morning. After the first lecture we had to split, I to Classical Art, and she to Art History. She was supposed to meet me at the cafeteria afterwards. I waited over an hour and she never pitched. She also didn't attend any of the afternoon classes we have together. Probably went for a fix."

"What is she taking?"

"Heroin. She showed me this morning. I wish I could help her, but she told me it's too late. How can I convince her to get help? It's never too late, right?"

"Right. Provided she wants to be helped." Joni handed him a glass of juice and sat down opposite the small coffee table from him.

"Did Tommy want to be helped?"

"I'm not sure, but apparently he's not doing too badly, doing his part. Isn't there someone to take care of Liza, to encourage her?"

"Only me. Her family lives across the continent from here, but they don't care anyway. So, forgive my impertinence, but why did you want to see her?"

"I rescued her twice from Tommy's claws and dropped her off here. That's how I know she lives here."

"I was wondering about that." Joni said this with a strange expression on her face and Quintin wondered about it. Before either of them could say anything, the door opened and Liza walked in, froze when she saw Quintin and asked uncertainly: "Hi, what ... ?" Quintin got up from his chair and said: "Hi, Liza, good to see you. I came looking for you. Didn't know you had a roommate."

"Why were you looking for me? You have news from Tommy?"

"Oh, yea. Tommy's doing okay. Looks like he'll be clean when he comes out."

"So, it's true. He is in rehab?"

"Yes. And it's doing him a lot of good. He'll be fine. So, how are you doing?"

"Fine. Thanks for asking."

"Well, I'd better be going. Just wanted to know if you're okay." Joni walked him to the door, but halfway he turned around and asked: "Wouldn't you girls like to attend a fun evening with me?"

"When and where?" They both looked eager.

"Friday night. At my church. Can I pick you up at six-thirty?"

"Church?" The girls looked at each other. If it were anyone else asking them, they would giggle and decline. But, with this guy they'll go anywhere.

"Sure, yea," said Joni.

"We'll be ready," added Liza.

"Great. See you Friday."

****

"Alright, Liza, now tell me. Where have you been all day?" Joni asked as soon as Quintin had left.

"What's this? Are you my mother now?"

"I'm your roomy and we had an appointment to meet for lunch."

"Sorry, couldn't make it. Anything else?"

"We got our assignments back."

"Did you bring mine? What symbol did I get this time?"

"Prof didn't give it to me. He asked me to tell you to go and see him. I suggest you go *asap*." Liza just pulled a face and asked: "What's to eat? I'm hungry?"

"I fried fish-fingers and warmed the onion and tomato mix. There's some leftover mash potato from yesterday also."

"On second thought, I'll just have a fruit and coffee." She delicately lifted a pear from the fruit basket on the kitchen counter and switched the kettle on.

****

Liza almost did not make it to Friday. Whether she wanted to be saved, or whether she was just negligent, Joni did not know. She was just very grateful that she found Liza's diary in time. It was Wednesday. Joni came home late from painting class. She had tried and tried again to make a perfect painting. Oil paint was the medium she felt most comfortable with, yet her best efforts were no better than mediocre. Deep in thought about her inability to create a great work of art, she entered the apartment. She called out for Liza, but the place was deafeningly quiet.

In the kitchen was a glass upside down in the drying rack. A banana peel lay on the counter next to the fruit basket. Joni picked it up and dropped it in the trashcan. Without any specific reason, she went to Liza's room. From time to time, Liza sorted out her stuff vigorously, tidying up to perfection, just to let it slip little by little until the room was in a mess again. Right then it was about in the middle of the cycle. A few items were lying around, but it was only moderately untidy. Joni's eyes wandered through the room until a little pale-green booklet caught her attention. It was lying half-buried under a bundled up tee-shirt on the bed.

Knowing it was Liza's diary, she felt a bit uneasy about opening it, even touching it. Curiosity got the better of her. She listened for footsteps, but all was still quiet. One quick step and she was by the bed, the booklet within reach. She grabbed it and, listening again, she opened the diary. Paging randomly through, there was nothing of significance. An inscription on Saturday's page drew her attention.

'The looks they like each other. Tommy is the small fish. Suitable for me. Or I for him. Let her have the big fish. She deserves him. Oh, but those eyes. How can I let the big fish go? Easy, coz I never had him'.

A bookmark was holding its place at the page of the previous day, Tuesday.

Enough. Tired of trying to do better. Tired of trying to quit the junk. Tired of being inferior. On the other side it will be better, must be better. If I can't get enough stuff from Penny tomorrow, I'll just jump.

Joni went cold. She knew it. It was in her eyes. Had been for days. She was going to do something to herself. Where is she? Where might she go? Suppose Penny didn't give her enough heroin to overdose? She might be standing on a bridge somewhere. Or looking down from a rooftop. "Oh, God," she cried out loud.

"What are you doing reading my diary!" Joni jumped at the angry voice of her roommate. She had not noticed her entering the apartment.

"I didn't meat to ... I mean I didn't ... Thank God you're home. Thank God you're safe. Liza. I was so worried about you." Liza grabbed the book from Joni's hand and threw it on the desk.

"Get out. I want to change." Joni just stood there, stunned: "Thank God you're safe," she repeated.

"I said get out!" Joni still did not move.

"Okay. You wanna stay and watch? I'll just change in front of you. Since we're both girls I suppose it doesn't matter. Just hope that none of our friends find us like this. They might think we have gone queer." Liza immediately started changing her clothes, but Joni hardly noticed, her eyes on every little pocket or pouch where drugs might be hidden.

"What are you gawking at? Never saw anyone changing before? Never saw your sister changing?" The tight jeans and skimpy blouse Liza was wearing, was now lying in a heap on the floor. Dressed in a pair of baggy, but comfortable sweatpants and a sweatshirt, Liza walked to the kitchen and switched on the kettle. Joni followed her and sat down on a barstool by the counter.

"Liza we need to talk. Please, tell me what's going on. Why are you ...? I read the last two inscriptions. Sorry if I intruded? But I'm glad I did. Just tell me about it."

"There's not much to say. I just sometimes like feel it's over for me. What's the purpose of everything. Why are we here? Where are we going from here? You know? It's like a cycle going nowhere. Getting born, eat, work, sleep, die, then what? So, why not end all this crap and get done with it?"

"And deprive the world of one of its greatest artists? Liza, you have so much potential. You're young. You can do things, go places, meet people. You have so much to give."

"Want coffee?"

"Course I want coffee."

"Anything more you want to say?"

"Friday Quintin is coming to pick us up."

"I'm not going. He wants you to go. He just invited me because he was polite."

"Wrong. He looked at you. I'm the one who will be tagging along, the fifth wheel."

"Nah, you're just saying it to make me feel better."

"Believe what you want. If you're not going, then I'm not going. Simple as that."

"Don't be ridiculous. You shall go."

"And so shall you." Liza smiled at that. For the first time in weeks, Joni saw a sparkle in Liza's eyes.

"Yea. So we both shall go. What would you like for supper?"

"Let's order. I'll pay."

They enjoyed a meal of pizza with almost everything on it, coleslaw and soft drinks and chatted like in the beginning when they first moved in together. Joni managed to relax a little concerning the things Liza wrote in her diary. Perhaps she did not mean it seriously. Perhaps she was just in a dark mood, and now it is over. Maybe she meant for Joni to find the diary and rescue her. But she will watch her roommate closely anyway. She won't let anything happen to her. Even if it meant that she had to get help.

Chapter 6

Change

Time passed too slowly for Joni. She studied hard, cleaned the apartment, did shopping, all just to kill time. Finally Friday dawned. She went through the regular routine of attending classes, eating lunch in the cafeteria did some practical work afterward, then hurried home to prepare for the evening. She could hardly contain her excitement by the thought of going out with Quintin. Though it was not a real date, she still looked forward to it. Even though she had to share him with Liza. She did not mind. Just the thought that she would be with him, made her feel warm all over.

Joni looked at her watch. Five twenty. Just as she started to worry about Liza, the door burst open and Liza stepped in.

"Have you made supper, or shall I?" she asked.

"I had a pie at the cafeteria. Just grab something and hurry up. Quintin will be here shortly." Liza pulled a face.

"I'm not going."

"Oh, yes you are. You promised him and you're not backing out. Have a sandwich and go get dressed."

"I told you no. So stop bugging me. You can have him all to yourself."

"You saw him first. Besides, he's not interested in us. Not in that way. Otherwise he would not have invited us both. Go on. I'm not taking no for an answer. I'll make you a sandwich while you're in the shower."

"Aww, you! Why can't you leave me alone!" Liza rolled her eyes and went to the bathroom. Joni quickly spread two slices of bread, grated some cheese on one slice, slapped a lettuce leaf on top, added a little sweet-chilly sauce, covered it with the second slice and cut the sandwich in half. She poured two cups of coffee and sat down by the kitchen counter, waiting for Liza to finish. Ten minutes later, Liza appeared, fresh as a daisy and hungry as a lion. She downed the food in two minutes. Quintin knocked on the door while Liza was brushing her teeth and Joni was looking in the mirror for the tenth time.

The two girls were quite nervous, not knowing what to expect from a fun evening at a church gathering, never before imagining to associate fun with church. They were both pleasantly surprised to see all the other young people dressed just like them, but showing less skin cheerfully greeting them as if they were the two long lost sisters. Though strange to church environment, they quickly felt at home and partook in the activities. If at first they felt uncomfortable during the opening prayer, they managed to hide it well. If anyone had noticed, no one showed it.

Following a short prayer of praise, thanksgiving and asking God's blessing on the gathering, the band started playing and everyone joined in the singing, praising and worshipping the Lord. The two girls were amazed, but joined in as best they could, and enjoying it.

"Right, guys and girls," Quintin said, "let's divide. Carl, you choose first." Carl, a tall skinny guy with sand colored hair and friendly green eyes pointed at Liza:

"New girl, what's your name again?"

"Liza."

"Right. Liza, come over here."

"I'll have the other new girl. Joni, please." And so Quintin and Carl divided the group to form two teams competing against each other. The girls did not do well during Bible quiz, but, of course, their teammates helped them, quietly whispering the answers. They were even worse at *Charades* because they did not know any Christian books, movies or anything else Christian. Again their teammates helped them. The time flew by with lots of laughter and, for the "new girls," lots of learning. They learned that Christians can have fun. Clean, sober fun without chemical stimulants. No need for earsplitting noise they used to call music. Fun without alcohol, pot or coke; possible? Fun without making out; possible? For the first time they realized it was possible.

"Okay, now let's break up into our regular groups before we conclude for the night." Quintin put a hand on Joni's shoulder saying: "I'll have you in my group. Carl, you take Liza again." Joni felt as if his hand burned a hole in her dress, overly aware of him again. During those final moments of prayer she hardly heard a word anyone prayed. She hardly noticed what was being prayed about. She was only experiencing Quintin's presence intensely. Sitting next to him with her eyes closed, he had to touch her arm before she realized prayer time had ended and the others were getting up to leave.

For Liza things worked out completely different. Carl took her by the arm and led her away to where his group was waiting. She felt different. She felt loved by each and all. For the first time in her life, she felt at home. When Carl asked if anyone had a special prayer request, she hesitated just for a moment. Then she pulled up her sleeve, turned the inside of her arm up for them all to see the needle marks where the heroine found entrance into her body. Shocked silence lasted only a second.

Carl motioned with his head to a girl named Connie, who stepped forward and lay both her hands on Liza's shoulders. The others joined, laying hands on her shoulders, her head, or just touching her arms or back with a hand or a finger.

Connie led them in prayer, some following in agreement, some softly whispering in unknown languages.

"How can I be like you? What must I do to, you know, get what you guys have?"

"You mean you wanna be a Christian?"

"Something like that I guess, yea."

"Liza, all you have to do, is confess your sins, ask Jesus to forgive you and hand over your life into His hands. In other words, trust Him in every situation, with every aspect of your life."

"Is that all? Is it really that simple?"

"Yes. That simple. And then you might wanna get baptized."

"When? Where?"

"Right now, if you are ready."

"I am ready."

****

At home, Joni walked on a pink cloud because Quintin had touched her, chose her for his team, invited her into his group, and touched her again. Liza walked on a pink cloud because she had met her Savior.

****

With summer approaching, the exams loomed ominously and the girls studied every night into the small hours. Friday evenings they attended the youth meetings with Quintin.

"C'mon, lazy bones, wake up." Liza opened one eye trying in vain to focus on the cup of coffee six inches from her nose.

"Go away, I'm sleeping."

"Nope, you're wide awake. Come now. Have your coffee and let's get started."

"Started on what? It's Saturday."

"Right. And what do we do on Saturday mornings? We clean."

"Not today, we don't."

"Oh, yes we do." Joni starts to be irritated now. "Come on Liza, get up now. The place is a mess and we won't have time to clean properly for a while. Exams starting on Tuesday and all that."

"You're a torturer." Liza moves, swung her feet off the bed and took the coffee that Joni had left on the night stand. She took a sip of the scalding hot liquid, put it down and went to the bathroom. Taking her time, the coffee had cooled enough to be gulped down in one breath. That was good, she thought. Joni knows how to make good coffee. She pulled her slender fingers through her unruly golden curls, dropped her night suit on the floor and pulled on an old sweat suit and canvas shoes.

"Reporting for duty, Ma'am."

"It's about time. There, grab a broom. You do the living room, I'll do the kitchen." With a groan, Liza obeyed, knowing the mood Joni was in, there was no getting away with sloppy work. She had better do a proper job, or Joni, on inspection will make her do it all over.

Two hours later the girls sat down in the living room each with a glass of fruit juice and a satisfied smile on their faces. Job well done, they could relax. It was still early and the mall was waiting. Liza took the empty glasses, rinsed them, dried them and put them away. Joni was already in the shower when she came out of the kitchen.

Freshly showered, dressed, make up carefully applied, they headed for the mall with no specific plans except to have brunch as they, having skipped breakfast, were both starving.

After a hearty meal, they strolled through the mall, doing a lot of window shopping, not so much real shopping. Two broke students on a Saturday morning getting away from their studies for a bit. They stopped at a jewelry shop. In the window were a number of beautiful pieces, lots of emeralds rubies and diamonds. An exceptionally remarkable ring caught Joni's eyes.

"Just look at that thing. Isn't that the ultimate?" She almost drooled on the shop window. "Oh, if only I could have it. I wish I had a rich boyfriend."

"Tell Quintin to sell more paintings. I'm sure he can afford it with the money from two or three paintings."

"Are you mad? He is not my boyfriend. I can't accept something like that from him, even if he could buy it, which I'm sure he can't."

"Well, then you have to forget about this little treasure and move on. Let's go." But Joni did not move. She kept on staring at the dainty design of the platinum ring with three small emeralds set in a curvy, curly setting, like tiny grapes on a vine.

"I want it. How long do you think will I have to work to get enough cash?"

"Forever."

"You are so discouraging. I'll get a summer job and earn enough for a deposit. You'll see."

"If you buy the ring, who's gonna pay your studies next year? Come on. You can't have it. Let's move."

"I want the ring." Joni kept on protesting.

"You know what, Joni? The first sin was not disobedience or rebellion, like some people think. It was coveting. Eve was disobedient when she bit into that fruit, but that disobedience was spawned when she coveted the wisdom the devil promised. You're coveting what you can't have right now. What unwise decisions do you think might come from your coveting this ring? If you wait a few years, finish your studies, get a good paying job, and maybe a rich boyfriend to go along, then you might be in a position to buy things like that. Just hang in there." Joni looked at her, astonished at this unexpected burst of wisdom. Not to mention the proper language usage.

"You're serious about this religion stuff, aren't you?"

"And you're not?" Liza looked at her friend challenging her to deny that she is in it for the sake of

Quintin and not for Jesus. But Joni just shrugged and started walking away.

"Let's go watch a movie," she said and Liza agreed.

****

With the exams a mere memory, summer holidays arrived with the promise of all sorts of good things. The girls agreed to take it easy for a week or two before they enter into the world of temporary employment. During this first week, Joni, dreading the thought, but having promised her mom, went home to spend some time with the family. Since her stepdad was in prison, it would not be so bad. She was very fond of her two younger brothers and missed them during the long academic year. Her older sister, Mandy was attending college in a different city and was not sure if she'd be home during the holiday. Joni's mother struggled financially, so the daughters had to work to provide for their own tuition. Mandy used it as an excuse, but the real reason was that she wanted to enjoy summer with her boyfriend.

Liza vowed never to return home. She and her mom were not close, and as her only sister was behind bars, there was no reason for her to go and she hadn't been home in two years.. To prevent trouble between Liza and the boyfriend, Liza's "stepfather", as Liza's mother preferred to call him, she did not encourage her to come home. Her choice was obvious. The "life partner" was more important.

****

Tommy was doing well in rehab. Quintin visited as often as he could, bringing him news from his father, who, for the best part ignored the boy. Though Quintin took it easy during summer, he still had to make some preparations for his next exhibition that was scheduled for early Fall. His visits to his young stepbrother was becoming less strained as the boy seemed to be maturing, finally. He was no longer rebellious and treated Quintin with respect.

Quintin usually spend the night in a motel as the drive out to the rehab center and back home, was too long and too tiring. At one such visit, Tommy's father invited him to stay over at his place, some hundred miles further away.

"Good to see you. Hope you don't mind driving all the way out here."

"Not at all, Sir," Quintin replied. "Are you well and everything okay?"

"Yes. Everything is fine. How is Tommy? I presume you saw him today?"

"I did. He seems fine. I hope it's not an act to get released earlier."

"You think it might be?"

"I'm not sure. He seems to be just a bit too subdued. Of course I hope I'm wrong. Perhaps he has really changed. It is almost four months."

"Well, it looks like you know him better than me. If you think he should stay longer, then so he shall. Because if he screws up one more time, I'm done with him. He's not a child anymore."

"I'll stop by his councilor on my way back. He was not available this morning and I'd like a word with him.

Just to get his opinion. If he confirms my suspicions, it will be at least two more months for Tommy. Why don't you come with me tomorrow?"

"Yea. Why not. But you do what you consider best. This is the only time I'm relieved that neither his mother, nor yours are around to see this day. I miss your mother, you know. I loved her. Edna was a great woman."

"I know. You told me that when Tommy's mother died, you were devastated."

"I was. With Tommy only three years old I didn't know what to do. I would not have coped. Then your mother came along and saved me. And you were like a real older brother to Tommy. That was why I adopted you and gave you the Trout name. I know I spoiled Tommy, but I didn't know what to do, how to raise him. He was so little when Josephine, his mother died. I was so sorry for him. People told me rather sorry when he is small and needed to be disciplined, than when he grows older and break my heart in a different way. This is exactly what is happening. It broke my heart to punish him when he was a small boy, and look what heartache I have to put up with now." Quintin did not know what to answer to that. It was obvious the man was suffering with guilt, and self-anger plaguing him.

They sat for a while in silence, Quintin finished his coffee, they said good night, each going to his room, the older man's glass of whiskey left untouched on the side table next to his easy chair.

****

Back at home Quintin reflected on his visit to Tommy and his stepfather. Tommy looked sincerely happy to see his father. No trace of the cynicism of the past. He was either a master actor or genuinely rehabilitated. It would be easy to believe the latter. So, why did he have this uneasy feeling about Tommy being released in two weeks?

Chapter 7

The Trap

The coffee shop where Liza worked as a waitress during the summer holidays was several blocks away from their apartment. Whenever she had the morning shift, she would walk wearing soft canvas shoes. For the afternoon shift, she took a bus. It was simply too hot to walk all the way and get there all sweaty and exhausted.

It was on this bright early morning shift that she was spotted. Two men were sitting in a booth when she appeared with a loaded tray from the kitchen.

"That's the one."

"You sure? Have you seen her before?"

"I told you. It's her. She's the one I saw with Tommy just before he disappeared into rehab."

"And you're sure she's the one stealing our customers by spreading the 'Good News' and get them to join her church?"

"Right again."

"Well now. We'll have to do something. We can't allow this pretty girl to go on in her sinful ways, can we?"

"What do you suggest?"

"Leave it to me. She doesn't know me. And you know how charming I can be."

"Yea," the guy grinned, "and how wicket too."

"Do you know Tommy's back in town?"

"No kidding?"

"The rumor's going that he is fully rehabilitated. Won't touch the stuff ever again."

"Oh, but we know better than to believe that. How many times did we hear that story, but it never proofs true. They always come back. Tommy will be back too. Just give him time."

"Which makes me think. Maybe we should help him along. And let him do the job on the girl. No fingers pointing at us."

"Good thinking. I like that."

"So, let's work out a plan."

"What if she converts him?"

"Nah, I know Tommy. He's beyond salvation. Especially if we offer a reward."

"And throw in a little warning if he doesn't play along."

"Yea, and I know just what kind of warning will do the trick." The two skunks finished their coffee and muffins and left the place in high spirits.

****

"Are you sure you want to do this, Tommy?"

"Yea, man. My dad needs me right now. We've never been close. This is a chance to pick up the pieces and glue them back together. I know he wants that too."

"I'm proud of you. Never thought I'd hear you say that, but I'm really glad for both of you. He can do with a little happiness. And so can you. Real happiness."

"Thanks. I'll just go say so long to a few guys and girls and then I'll come packing my stuff. I can hardly wait for Saturday to get outa here."

"Fine. Just stay away from the old crowd. Say good bye to the good friends. Will you see Liza also?"

"She's the only girl I want to see."

"Right. Off you go then. Don't come back too late." Tommy just smiled and left the apartment Quintin shared with him for more than two years.

He felt light hearted at the prospect of seeing Liza after so many months. He sort of grew fond of her. Not only for what he could get from her. She really was a nice girl. Turning a corner two blocks from her apartment, the ambush was waiting.

"Hey, Tommy, good to see you, man. What's up?" Tommy stopped walking, not knowing what to do, where to go.

"Phil, Stan. Hi, ... "

"I heard you were out. Been waiting for your call, but nothing happened. Are we cool?"

"Yea, we're cool."

"Then you won't mind walking with us?"

"Err, well, guys, I ... "

"C'mon, Tommy, just a little walk down a city street with two old friends. Two best friends? What harm can that do?"

"Right. But I don't have much time. Quintin is watching me and ...."

"Yea, man, big brothers are always watching. They watch us do good things, and they watch us getting in trouble. What can they do?"

"Sometimes we watch them getting into trouble and what can we do? Hey? Come along now like a good boy. You don't want big brother getting into some kind of mess, do you?"

"What do you mean? You better leave Quintin alone."

"Or what? What you gonna do? Rescue him? You?" They laughed out loud and ugly. They took both Tommy's arms and dragged him along, Tommy's mind spinning. Inside a building, they forced Tommy through a door and told him to sit down. He took a seat at a small table in the middle of the floor. A short, skinny man, dark skinned, with thick black, wavy hair that starts an inch above his eye brows, entered and took the seat at the table opposite Tommy. In a hoarse, smokers voice, he addressed the young man in front of him:

"Tommy, Tommy. By taking you away, your brother caused us to lose a lot of money. We should be collecting from him to cover our losses. Hmm? I mean, breaking his bones wouldn't do any good. Because then he can't deliver no more. Or do you think we should break his bones? Just to get even for what he did to you, putting you in a difficult situation like this? Hmm?"

"No, please, don't hurt him. He meant well. He ... "

"Shut up. You talk when I say you talk. Now, Tommy baby, this is how it's goi'n be. You bring us the girl and we leave big bro alone. That girlfriend of yours is causing us a lot more trouble than Quintin ever could. You know, that nice blondie, curly top that used to buy the good stuff from us. Now she goes around tell'n everyone to follow Jesus. Quit the stuff and go to church, that's what she's tell'n our customers. Naughty girl, that one. So, we're goi'n to have to reprimand her. You bring her and we convince her, okay? Make sure she's at the Goose tonight. Eight 'o clock." He handed Tommy a small bottle and gestured with his hands what he wanted Tommy to do with it, pour the liquid in Liza's drink. "Be there, or big bro won't walk on two legs again."

Tommy walked away in the direction of Quintin's apartment. His mind is spinning, not knowing what to do. He can't betray Liza. She is so cute, so breakable, so ... so ... . No, he can't and he won't. But then what? They'll go for Quintin. They will break his knees, or worse, his hands and he'll never paint again. Liza or Quintin. Liza or Quintin. How is he supposed to choose? Either one or the other? No, no, no! He loved Liza. He owed Quintin. He needed a cold beer right now. But he can't have one. He should jump off a bridge, but he is scared of heights. He can OD, but they'll find Liza, or Quintin, or both anyway. Only he, Tommy, can save them. Sorry, sad, pathetic Tommy must save them. He didn't need a beer. He needed a plan. He was in a hurry now, to get home, clear his head and make a plan. There was no other way. He had to get them away, out of town.

He flung open the door and called out to Quintin. He had to be there. No reply. He called louder. Silence. No!. He can't leave without him. He took out his cell phone and dialed:

"Tommy? What's up? You okay?"

"Yea I'm okay. You? Where are you?" Tommy tried to sound normal, but he knew he didn't.

"I'm at the airport. You sure you're okay?"

The Bigger Fish

"Why are you at the airport?"

"I told you last week I'm going to Chicago for a few days. Listen, Tommy, if you have a problem I'll cancel and come back right home. Tell me what's going on."

"No! I'm fine. I thought you're going next week. That's great. Enjoy Chicago. Stay as long as you want. Take a vacation. Have a great trip. Call me when you land."

"You sure you're okay?"

"Sure I'm sure. Relax, I'm fine. No funny stuff. I promise. Hey, I gotta go. Talk later."

Tommy parked his car close to the coffee shop where Liza worked. He has some vague idea of how to implement his plan. He walked in, sat down in a booth and waited for Liza to come and take his order.

"Tommy! What a surprise. I heard you were back. You okay?"

"Yea. I'm okay. You?"

"Fine. I'd like to talk to you, but right now I have to take your order or get fired."

"Bring me two milkshakes, bubblegum flavor."

"Two? You waiting for someone?"

"Yea, you. The second shake is for you. I'm sure you can spare a minute for an old buddy." She giggled and, looking to see if the boss was watching, whispered:

"Okay, but just for a minute." That's all I need, he thought, just one minute. Liza returned with the milkshakes and sat down. Tommy started coughing violently.

"Bring me some water, please," he managed through gasps and coughs. The moment she left, he poured half of the contents of the tiny vial that was given him by 'Mr Threatscare', into her shake and stirred. He took the glass eagerly and gulped down half of the water.

"I told my boss I need a break and he gave me five minutes. So tell me all there is to tell. Do it quickly because I have a lot to tell you."

"I don't have much. And who wants to hear about rehab anyway. So, you go ahead.

"All right, well, you see, I'm clean too. And without rehab. I found Jesus, or He found me, rather. My life will never be the same. I'm clean, I'm free, I have joy. That is something I didn't even know existed. I was never joyful. I was like seriously considering ending it all, you know. And then He changed me. I'm a new creature. I'm not the Liza you knew before."

"I can see that. It's all over your face. You're different." For a moment he was enthralled, but, taking a sip of his milkshake, he remembered why he was there in the first place. He motioned for Liza to drink her shake, worried for a moment that she might not want it and the liquid from the vial would be wasted. How will he get her out? She won't be convinced that her health was in serious danger if she stayed. Of course he couldn't tell her. He breathed deeply with relief when she finally put the straw to her mouth and started sucking.

Chapter 8

Liza

Back from Chicago after two days, Quintin opened his front door just to find the place in a mess. Drawers plucked out, the contents strewn all over the place. A vase broken on the floor. Same thing in the kitchen. Even groceries laying everywhere. He stepped carefully over some papers, dropped his bag and reached for his phone when he saw the broken window behind the sofa.

Careful not to disturb anything, he inspected the apartment so see what was stolen. To his surprise nothing was missing. When the police came, it was their opinion that it could have been addicts who thought they might find drugs. They asked if Quintin was using, whether his roommate was using, to which he could truthfully say no. They took his report, promised to find the culprits, a promise Quintin did not take seriously, and left. He thought of calling Tommy, but why worry him if nothing was stolen and he was not about to return soon.

Let him have his time with his father as long as he was needed. Time to clean up the mess.

It was late afternoon when he was finished cleaning up. The owner of the building promised to have the window replaced the next day. He'll have to board it up for the night. Although tired, he did not want to spend the evening there. He needed to relax, get out and have a nice meal. And he did not want to do that alone. He dialed Joni's number. Engaged. He tried again after a few minutes, noticing there were two missed calls, but decided to check them after he called Joni.

"Hi Joni, it's Quintin. How you do'n?"

"Quintin, hi. Did Tommy phone you?"

"No, why do you ask?"

"He ... he just called me, he ... " She sounded distressed and Quintin was worried now.

"What did he say? ... Joni, talk to me ... "

"H he said ... it's Liza ... oh, can you please come over?"

"I'm on my way." By the time he ended the call he was already running down the stairs on his way to his car.

She opened the door and when he saw her face, ashen with shock and fear, his heart sank into his shoes, expecting the worst. He reached out with his hands on her shoulders drawing her closer. With both hands she grabbed hold of his shirt and started crying. He held her close to his heart, stroking her hair while her tears stain his shirt. When the sobbing subsided, he held her away, dried her tears and led her to the sofa. It was time to tell.

"Tommy called me just before you did. He said there was some accident with a horse. He wasn't clear on what exactly happened, but it looks like Liza broke her neck.

She's dead, Quintin ... she ... ". The tears streamed again and Joni could not complete her sentence.

"There, there," he patted Joni gently on the back holding her in one arm.

"Is that all he said?" She nodded.

"Yea. He talked some more, but he seemed to be in shock. I couldn't understand any detail he was trying to give me."

"Where are they?"

"I'm not sure. He said something about his dad's ranch, but, I just don't know. Maybe you should call him. Perhaps he'll explain better to you." He already had his cell phone out and dialing.

"Tommy, I'm with Joni. What's going on, what happened?"

"Liza. She fell off Dad's horse and broke her neck. It was a freak accident. She shouldn't have been hurt. It happened so quickly. One moment she was mounting, the next she started sliding off on the other side, fell on her head and broke her neck. She was doing so well, learning fast."

"Where was your dad?"

"He was right there, with us, less than ten meters from her. I was supposed to keep her safe. I was supposed to protect her. I ... I don't know what so say. I thought she'd be safe on the ranch."

"Why do you say that? Why did you take her with you? What would she be safe from?"

"Can't tell you on the phone. We'll talk when I get back".

"Where is your dad now?"

"Napping. He was given something for the shock."

"You're not coming back for a while. Stay with the original plan. Your dad needs you now, more than ever. I'll see how soon I can be there." He did not know why, but his insides were telling him something.

"Can you get time off from your summer job?" he asked Joni.

"I'm only starting next week. I just got back from a visit home, so I postponed my job. Why?"

"Go pack a bag. We're going to the ranch. And we're leaving now."

They drove through the night and reached the ranch in the early hours. Tommy opened the door and offered coffee so they would not disturb Tommy's father. Tired as anything, Quintin would not hear of going to bed before he heard the full story. There by the kitchen table Tommy told everything about the threat from the drug lieutenant, how he spiked Liza's milkshake so he could get her out of town and out of reach. He would have done that to Quintin too if he was not going to Chicago for a few days.

"And what happened with the horse?" Tommy slowly moved his head from side to side.

"People fall off galloping horses without getting badly hurt. This horse was standing there like a statue. It was in front of the barn, on the cobble stone pavement. She got on, like she'd been doing expertly for two days. Kept on practicing till she got it right. She loved the horses. You'd never know she hadn't been on a horse before. And then, yesterday, just after lunch she wanted to go riding again." Tommy kept on shaking his head.

"Can't believe it. She got on the horse the usual way, then slowly starting to slide off on the other side. I thought she was going to correct herself. We both started laughing, you know. It looked so funny. But suddenly she toppled over, landed on her head and I was waiting for her to say something. I ran to help her up. She was limp, she was not responding when I spoke to her. She just moved her eyes, it looked like she was trying to smile. And then … then she lay still, her eyes staring at nothing. Her breathing had stopped. I held her and yelled for Dad to get help. I held her until the medics came. They declared her dead right there."

The silence that followed was as thick and black as the night outside. Neither Quintin nor Joni knew what so say. After many minutes Quintin broke the silence:

"Have you contacted her folks?"

"No, dunno where they are. Joni, do you know?"

"I don't. She hardly ever spoke about them. But I'm sure there are contact details at the apartment. I'll have a look in her room as soon as I get home." Joni spoke the last few words with quivering lips and an unsteady voice.

"Where is her cell phone? You could probably find something there."

****

Joni was back in her apartment. Alone. Her cheerful, girly roomy will never return. Quintin dropped her off an hour earlier, tired after the long drive back from the ranch. They spent a day with Tommy and his dad, making sure they were both okay. It was arranged that Liza's body would be transported to her home town. Her mother promised to come and get Liza's things after the funeral. Joni was to pack everything, so there would not be any delay. Some more arrangements were made before Quintin and Joni returned. They left very early in the morning, before the sun was up, and drove all the way back, only stopping for a bathroom break, gas and a bite to eat.

They reached Joni's apartment late in the afternoon. He carried her bag and put it down in the living room. Then he turned, cupped her head in his hands, pulled her closer and gently kissed her on the lips. They held each other for long minutes before he let go, closed the front door behind him and left. His footsteps, as he walked away, was the loneliest sound Joni had ever heard.

She couldn't get herself to even open the door to to Liza's room. Tomorrow is when she will do it, she told herself. After a strong cup of coffee, she took a shower, went straight to bed and cried herself to sleep, whispering Jesus, why? Jesus, help me.

She woke up before dawn. Rubbing her eyes, she could not believe that she slept for twelve hours. Crawling out of bed, she went to the kitchen to make herself a cup of coffee. With steaming liquid in one hand, she opened the door of Liza's room with the other. Inside, Joni stood staring at everything. She tried to take in every little detail as it was. It was not hard to imagine how Liza moved around in the room, dropping a shoe here, leaving a t-shirt there, sitting on the bed leaving a dent in the middle. The bed was not even made up neatly, the sheets and blanket just pulled up to the pillows to show there was an effort.

Finishing her coffee Joni looked for a place to start sorting the stuff out. Study books on one side of the desk, all other study material on the other side. It was easier to work with the books than the personal stuff like clothes, make-up and so forth. But eventually she had to tackle the clothes. First she gathered the laundry, placed it in the basket, then folded and sorted and placed in neat heaps on the bed, together what belonged together.

Clothes stacked in tidy rows on the bed, Joni moved on to the closet and went through the shelves and drawers to sort out the sparse jewelry and nik-naks of all kinds. All very personal stuff. She remembered Liza buying some of the things, how they argued, Joni telling her it didn't match any of her outfits, or it looked kind of kitsch, or childish. But Liza liked childish, or child-like things, girly things. It was as if she held on to those things to somehow retain a sort of symbolism of a childhood lost too soon to the lusts of a pedophilic stepfather.

With a handful of pink and purple hairclips, Joni sat on the only open spot on the bed and started crying again. A life so full of promise, gone. With talents so intense and unique, now lost. Joni dried her tears and went to the kitchen for some more coffee. Contemplating the events of the last few days, Joni sat at the kitchen table, staring at nothing, trying to imagine exactly how Liza died. What really happened on that horse that made her fall? Why couldn't she stop herself from landing on her head? What was her last thoughts? Did she really try to smile, as Tommy said, or was it more of a grimace? Did she know she was dying? How did she feel about dying? How do I feel about dying? A million questions, no answers.

She finished her coffee, now cold, rinsed her cup and went back to Liza's bedroom. The sky in the east is slowly turning grey. The work had to be done by the time sunshine hits the pavement. She emptied the drawers and shelves methodically, placing the things neatly on the dresser. Halfway through the process, a small booklet fell on the floor from among some notebooks and diaries from previous years. Joni picked it up and curiously started paging through the book.

It was not exactly a diary, although at some inscriptions there was a date added at the bottom of the page. She read random pieces scattered throughout the book.

Tommy is a liar.

Wish Penny would leave me alone. She's dragging me down. I can feel it. She is dragging me down.

Classes sucked today. Couldn't wait for practical.

If I don't get it right tomorrow, I'll never touch a paint brush again.

Tommy is a doll. Just gotta luv da guy. Small fish, but so am I. We're a match

When is Joni going to take me seriously? Joni pulled in her breath. When did she not take Liza seriously? She read on:

Saw Mr Browneyes today. What a hunk. Big fish to catch.

Tommy is a skunk. His stuff was cut.

At last. Now I can call myself a painter. Even old Me Paintbrush is impressed. My painting deserves a place in the Louvre.

Test results, uhg. Will I ever graduate? Wish I was like Joni. Always organized. Always prepared. Tears streamed down Joni's cheeks. How many times did I wish I had half of your talent, Liza?

Shame drowns me. Rescued by Mr Browneyes. I always knew I was not good enough for him. But now he knows about me. How will I ever show my face in public again? Dying might be an option.

Got a C+ for Art History. Life is good.

Stuck a needle in my arm last night. It was great. And now I hate myself.

Missing Tommy. Going for the needle again tonight.

Miserable

Miserable times 10.

Joni, do you see me?

If I don't end it today, I'll go crazy.

Date with Browneyes? Great. Even if Joni and I have to share him.

Can't go through. Have to make an end.

The day my life changed. Browneyes Quintin showed me the way. Always knew he would change my life. Wasn't really him, it was HIM. Jesus. Jesus, Jesus. You really, really changed me. I am new. I am clean. I am free. I love you. I will serve you forever.

Why does Joni see Quintin and not Jesus? Q. is a great guy, but Jesus is the ONE, the bigger fish.

Jesus, open Joni's eyes, let her see.

Quintin is blocking Joni's vision. Lord, don't take him from her, just make her see past him.

Jesus, please, save Joni, whatever it takes, so she can be free like me. So she can have joy like I have. She can't be allowed to die without You. Whenever she dies, Lord, she's gotta be with you. I'm so looking forward to seeing you face to face. And she's gotta be there too. She's gotta be there. And if I go before Joni, I want her to have all my study materials, my sketches, paintings and all my art equipment and materials. My clothes go to Sis, hopefully she'll be out by then, or not back in. All the rest, the little cash I might have at the time, can go to some charity.

Joni could hardly read the last words through her tears. Sobs shuddered her body. When her stomach was sore and the well of tears have dried up, she sank down on her knees:

"Jesus, let Liza's prayers be answered. Wash me, make me clean, make me free, make me new, inside out. Forgive my sins, forgive me for giving Quintin priority over you. Come, take over my life and give direction. I don't know how to cope with this. Give me strength and hope and courage. Come, Jesus. Take over."

****

"Joni, did something happen? You look different."

"I am different. I'm new, I'm clean, I'm free. I have joy like never before." He smiled broadly, inviting her into his apartment later that day when she knocked on his door.

"I can see you want to tell me about it." She sat down on the other side of the coffee table across from him. Taking a sip of the fruit juice he handed her, she told him all about the little note book, what she had read in it and what happened afterward. For Quintin, it was the best day in a long time.

****

Joni, Quintin and Tommy went together to attend Liza's funeral. Tommy's reason to attend was quite different from theirs. He was there to punish himself for not protecting Liza. He was her savior and he failed. Handing her over to the drug lieutenant would damage her, but she'd still be alive. Which would have been worse, sudden death, or torture and rape and the return to the needle? The situation seemed hopeless.

For Quintin and Joni it was sad, but at the same time a joyful event. Quintin told it all in his eulogy:

"We will miss Liza, but we know she is not dead. We know she is forever in a place where no harm can ever come to her again". No lustful stepdad can touch her again, no needle can enter her blood vessels again and no drug lieutenant can torture her. This, he only thought, but didn't say.

"She was in the place where every child of God long to be at the end of his time. Liza's life with Jesus on earth was short, but it will last to eternity. She loved Him, served Him with every fiber in her body and every piece of her soul. The joy that shone from her was lighting up the lives of everyone she came across. Liza, wait for us. Someday in the, hopefully not so near future, we'll see you again."

Chapter 9

Tommy

The drug ring did not forget about Tommy. Especially the fact that he did not obey their orders. They told him to bring Liza and he did not. He tried to hide her. Too bad she got killed. They had so much fun in mind for her. But now Tommy will have to have the fun. He became very evasive, but they will find him. They knew all his hangouts. And they knew he will not stay away.

Tommy did not forget about the drug ring and their threats. He knew that, since Liza was dead, they would focus on him. Avoiding his old hangouts was not a problem. He was done with them anyway. No more using, no more rehab. Going clean from now on. But he knew if they really wanted him, they would find him easily. His dad needed him, but, what if they found him on the ranch and endangered his father? They were resourceful and they had enough money to trace him anywhere. Time to make a new plan. A plan that must involve Quintin.

****

It was Phil and Stan's job once more to get Tommy. They traced him, watched him, then, as soon as they were sure of his routine, waited in ambush.

"Tommy, my man. Great to see you. Where you been?" Tommy froze in his tracks, held up his hands as if in surrender.

"Hey, guys, I er, I ... "

"C'mon, buddy, don't waste our time. Come along like a good boy. The big man is waiting." Just like before, they dragged him into the same building as before and pushed him down into the same rickety chair. The door opened and two men entered. One was the same guy that made the threats a couple of weeks earlier. The other one looked even scarier. He was not tall, but stocky, with a neck the size of any average young bull. His pale blue eyes were small and beady and continuously moving. He had a round, shaved head, a mouth full of bad, yellowed teeth and a nasty grin on his face. Mr Threatscare was the talker, the other guy, the one with the round head, was the knee breaker.

"Now, Tommy, you've been a very naughty boy. The boss is not happy. Liza is gone, but we wanted to make an example of her. You know. Show the world what happens to people who try to sabotage our business. You took that opportunity away from us. What do you think we should do now? Don't you think it would be fair to us if we expect you to replace her? Don't you think it would be justice if you stand in for her? I mean, the world's gotta know, you know. People's gotta respect us. You and your girl took away people's respect for us. Now you gotta earn it back for us."

"Anything, sir. Just say what I need to do." They looked at each other and burst out laughing, loudly and ugly.

"Oh, you wanna help us now? Well. Let me tell you how it's gonna be, Tommy. Manny here is gonna break you in two. And then he's gonna throw both pieces in the river. That way people will know not to mess with Big Mikey. That way you'll earn us back people's respect. Manny, ... " Big Mikey motioned with his eyes towards Manny, the knee breaker.

It was his last words that provided the cue. And it would be the last words he would ever speak. Police stormed in from every side. Big Mikey, or Mr Threatscare, as Tommy called him in his thoughts, pulled a gun on himself and blew his own brains out. Manny was arrested and joined Phil and Stan who were already cuffed and waiting in the police van. Pity about Big Mikey. He would have been able to provide the police with the big names. It was doubtful if Manny knew any higher-ups. Like Phil and Stan, he was just a goon that took orders. Still, now that they knew who Big Mikey was, they might be able to find something by digging deeper into his past and his circles.

Tommy was patted on the back for his courage to let himself go wired into the lion's den. He was delivered back to Quintin who was waiting anxiously at the police station. Together they went back to Quintin's apartment. The next day Tommy returned to the ranch to help his dad finalize arrangements for the auction. His dad's health urged him to sell the ranch for something smaller and less challenging. He was already looking for a place closer to Tommy and was actually looking forward to settle for less stress and to provide a place for Tommy to come home over weekends.

****

The stress and strain of the month following Liza's death, the breaking up of the drug ring and his father's belief that Tommy was a hero, took its toll. Still mourning Liza, whom he seriously had fallen in love with, still looking over his shoulder for the next drug thug to grab him, on top of living up to his father's expectations, he had to crash. He was not as strong suddenly as everyone expected him to be. Deep down he was still weak, pathetic Tommy. That was his belief. He needed a crutch, something to make him strong, help him believe in himself the way others did. Penny can help him with that.

With his father settled in his new place an hour's drive from the city, the new academic year a week ahead, Tommy drifted. He was back with Quintin in the apartment and felt restless while his stepbrother went about his business. Finally he could not help himself anymore. He dialed a number.

"Hi, Penny, it's me, Tommy. How you doin?"

"Tommy! What do you want?"

"I was wondering. Could I see you sometime?"

"What for? We have noth'n to discuss."

"Come on, Penny, just once."

"I think you're crazy, Tommy, crazy to call me. I'm hang'n up."

"Wait, Penny, ... " but the phone was dead. He dialed again.

"Penny, don't hang up. Listen, I really need to see you. You know what I mean? There's no one that can help me. Please."

"I'll call you back. Sit tight." Tommy waited half an hour and almost changed his mind. Then his phone vibrated.

"Meet me at the Goose at nine." Before Tommy could reply, the phone was dead. Nervously he prepared for the evening.

He was not prepared for the dressing down he received from Penny before she, reluctantly, handed the small packet of white powder over to him. She asked him how he dared expect any trader to trust him after what happened to Big Mikey. Of course he denied any involvement. She told him vehemently what a risk she took to help him out. Everybody suspected him and he'd better watch out. Back at home he made sure Quintin was out for the night. He got his equipment ready when the phone rang. Oh, no, not now. It was his father. He'd better answer, you never know. The old guy never called this late. He should be in bed sleeping. This could only spell trouble.

"Hi Dad, what's wrong?"

"Tommy, I'm sorry to bother you this late," a groan followed before his father continued: "I fell and hurt my back. My leg is also sore. Just thought I'd let you know. Sorry to bother you."

"Dad, how serious is it? Did you get help? Must I come over?"

"No, I'm sure I'm okay. I took some pain pills and I'm in bed now. I just thought I'd let you know." Tommy heard another groan and then a sound as if something fell."

"Dad! You okay? What fell? I heard something falling."

"It's only my reading glasses. I bumped it off the night stand. Don't worry. Go to bed now. I'll call again in the morning."

"You sure? I can come over if you need me."

"No, Tommy, I'll cope. You can't come running every time I have an ache. College is starting soon and then you must focus on your studies." By the end of the sentence his father sounded out of breath. Then Tommy heard another groan, louder this time.

"Good night, Tommy. Call you in the morning," he said after a pause. Tommy sat by his table, undecided. He looked at the white powder, then at his phone. Be a man once in your life, he told himself. He grabbed the small sachet, emptied the contents into the toilet and flushed. He put the equipment away, called Quintin to let him know, then grabbed his car keys and made for the door. He reached his father's place before one in the morning.

When Quintin and Joni arrived the next morning, they found Tommy asleep in a chair, next to his father's bed at the local hospital. He had found his father in bad shape and called for an ambulance right away. He followed in his car and stayed by his dad throughout the night. Just before dawn, exhaustion got the better of him and he fell asleep.

The next day there was a short report in the newspaper about a girl who had been found in her apartment. She had died of an overdose. There was pure, uncut heroine found in her body. Very unusual. Tommy recognized Penny in the photo and read the whole report. He might never find out that the uncut stuff was meant for him, but he appreciated the fact that he had escaped the same fate. Jesus, You really are alive. You protected me. You used my dad's injury to keep me from using that stuff. Thank You Jesus. Thank You. Now I know Liza was right, Quintin and Joni are right. You are real.

Two days later the doctor declared Ted Trout fit to be dismissed and Tommy took him home. He stayed with him the rest of the week and convinced him to appoint a nurse to live in and take care of him. At least for the time being. This arrangement worked out extremely well for Ted, better than expected. The mother of the nurse stopped by one day, was invited to have tea and a romantic relationship began. A month later, the nurse was fired and her mother moved in as Mrs. Ted/Anne Trout.

Chapter 10

Caught

The academic year started with both Tommy and Joni jumping in, full force. As before, Joni tried her best at the practical work, but concentrated on the theoretical subjects where she scored excellent grades.

Life in general was tough for Joni. She could not find a replacement for Liza. Having to pay the full rent for the apartment, forced her to take on another part time job. She ate little, lost weight and by Thanksgiving she was skinny as a fashion model. Quintin urged her to try and find another roommate, but she was reluctant. Liza as a person was irreplaceable. As a roommate, well, as she explained it to him, was easy to get along with. Joni just did not have the energy to adapt to another stranger. She made Liza's room into a study room for herself. All her art equipment, and study materials were packed neatly into the shelves.

Among her things, she found the remains of that sketch Liza made of Quintin the day they saw him at the art gallery. She put all the little pieces together, those that survived the trash can, glued them onto a card board and had the picture framed. She hung it on the wall above the desk in honor of the late artist, Liza Cowan. She soon became aware that the picture was distracting. While sitting at the desk studying, she would look up to the picture too often, her thoughts drifting away from her studies. The only solution to this problem was to move the desk to a position where her back was turned to the picture. That worked out fine and she continued to make perfect grades.

She worked hard, studied hard, but Friday evenings were reserved for the youth meetings she attended with Quintin faithfully. After the meetings, Quintin sometimes took her out for a proper meal, but often she was too tired. On such evenings he ordered pizza or Chinese to be delivered to her apartment, made coffee and just chilled with her until she started yawning. He would then rinse their cups, clean the kitchen, kiss her on the forehead, push her in the direction of her bedroom and close the front door behind him.

****

Joni did not go home for Christmas. No money, she explained to her mother, who accepted the reason as valid, forever having to battle the money monster herself. Quintin invited her to a party on Christmas Eve, but Joni wanted to work. Jumping up from the easy chair in her living room, he grabbed her by the shoulders, lifted her chin with one hand and looked her in the eyes.

"No, Joni, you're not going to work on Christmas Eve. You're burning out, you're skinny as a skeleton and there are dark circles round your eyes. You're taking two days off and get some rest. That is what holidays are for. Not for working harder." She wanted to be angry, wanted to scream at him, ask him who gave him permission to rule her life, but she was too tired. She merely managed a nod, her lips quivering at his concern. He cupped her head in both his hands and placed a tender kiss on the triangle between her eyes and her nose. He left without another word. As usual when he touched her, chills chased each other up and down her spine.

On Christmas Eve Quintin picked her up and drove to the party at a friend's house. The next day, Christmas Day, he collected her for the early service at his church. Afterward, she agreed to accompany him to his stepfather's to spend the rest of the day with them. Tommy was already there. Anne, Ted's new wife was the perfect hostess and treated them like royalty. The meal was a feast and the atmosphere was festive, but relaxed. When they left late in the afternoon, they were made to promise to visit again soon.

It was a changed Joni who got out of his car after the visit. She was relaxed, a trace of pink on her cheeks, a new sparkle in her eyes. Her holidays were not over. Quintin left her, telling her to be ready by midmorning when he was going to take her out for brunch.

The next morning Joni got out of bed when the sun was high in the sky. After a slow cup of coffee, she took a long, warm shower and dressed with care, making an effort to look her best. The result must have been spectacular because Quintin's face showed nothing but amazed appreciation. After a hearty meal they strolled through the shopping mall, doing window shopping and chatting about nothing important.

Doing some window shopping they strolled from store to store, holding hands as they went. Joni stopped at the same jeweler where she saw the fabulous ring over which Liza reprimanded her about coveting. The ring was no longer there, but there was another one that she liked just as much. This time, however, she did not make a fuss. She did not even mention it. But Quintin watched her closely.

"What are you looking at?" He asked the question casually, as if it did not matter much.

"Oh, just a few nice pieces." She told him about the ring she saw months ago and how Liza preached a whole sermon to her. He chuckled at her animated account of the incident, which made her giggle. Suddenly tears filled her eyes.

"I miss her so much, you know."

"I know. She was a very special girl." He held her by the shoulders and kissed her on that special place where her nose and her eyebrows come together. They walked on to the next shop and the next and then they stopped at a coffee shop to give their feet some rest. Joni excused herself to pay a visit to the restroom. The moment she disappeared from his sight, he stole away quickly, quietly and went back to the jeweler. Before she reappeared, he was back in his seat and talking to the waitress. They ordered tall mugs of Brazilian coffee and apple crumble with whipped cream.

It was late afternoon when Quintin discovered that he had "left his cell phone somewhere". He asked Joni to wait for him while he jogged back to the coffee shop in search for his phone. He did not go to the coffee shop, because his phone was in his pocket. He passed the coffee shop, went straight to the jeweler, paid for the neatly wrapped parcel and jogged back to where Joni was waiting.

Leaving the mall, they stopped in their tracks in surprise. It had started snowing earlier and the parking lot was covered in white. Quintin drove away, but not in the direction of either of their apartment blocks. He drove on past the college, past downtown and pulled over next to a beautiful park with trees and little benches hidden behind snow covered shrubs. He opened the car door and helped her out. Arm in arm they strolled along a narrow path, snowflakes accumulating on their hair and shoulders.

At one of the little hidden benches he sat down and pulled her down next to him. He turned so that he could look directly into her face, taking both her hands in his.

"Joni, you know, I like you. Actually, I do more than just like you." A tenderness crept into her eyes as she looked back at him. He pulled her closer, cupped her face in his hands and kissed her on the lips, first gently, and as she responded, the kiss grew intimate, her lips parting slightly, her arms tightly circling his body. When he finally let go, they were both out of breath and feeling weak around the knees.

"I love you, pretty girl. I want you to always remember that." He pulled a small parcel from his pocket and placed it her hand. She unwrapped it, opened the tiny black, velvet box and gasped for breath. Snow accumulated on the dainty ring in the box before she found her voice and the right words to whisper.

"This is the most beautiful thing I've ever seen. Oh, Quint, is it really for me?"

"Since there is no one else in the park, I guess it is."

"I don't know what to say." He gently took the ring from the box and drew her left hand towards him.

"Say 'yes' just say 'yes' and then kiss me." He carefully pushed the ring on her left hand ring finger.

"'Yes' to what question?" She asked, teasingly.

"'Yes' to 'will you marry me?'." She looked at her ringed finger, then into his eyes and said softly but clearly: "Yes, Quintin, I'll marry you. You caught me, line, hook and sinker."

"Nope. I'm the 'Trout', the fish that you got in your net."

****

A week after Joni and Tommy graduated from college, Quintin put his luggage in the trunk of his car and drove to Joni's apartment for the last time. He collected her luggage, loaded it in the trunk of his car and opened the passenger door for her. He drove to his stepfather's house where he kissed Joni good bye and left for the nearby guest house where he had reserved a place for himself for the night.

It was a small, intimate reception in the garden among the roses, where the blooms were still covered in dew. The bride looked sweeter than honey in a pale peach colored dress that accentuated the coppery brown of her hair. A more radiant bride had not been seen in a while, neither a groom showing more white teeth.

By lunch time, the groom announced their departure and the couple started greeting the guests. A special thanks to Mr. Trout and his wife for the lovely wedding they had organized at their home, and to Joni's mother sister and brothers who made the effort to attend. And then Mr. Quintin Trout took Mrs. Joni Trout by the hand, waved one more time and left the party. They had a long drive to the log cabin by the lake where they would honeymoon for a week.

Entering the town at the edge of the lake, Quintin stopped to pump gas. He drove to a coffee shop for a light meal before he had to set the GPS in search for the cabin village. He placed their order and while they waited for their coffee and food, he took out a flat parcel from a bag and placed it in front of Joni on the table. One more surprise took her breath away. It was like looking back six months into the past. She could remember her feelings when he put that ring on her finger. Here, in this painting he managed to portray exactly, on her face, the feelings she had at that moment. It was a small painting of a snow covered park with two people on a park bench, the man holding the hand of the girl, the ring on her finger.

"When did you make this painting?" she asked still amazed.

"While you were cramming for the finals."

"Oh, Quint, you keep on surprising me. What a lovely painting. It is as if you made it from a photograph. Precisely as it was, that day when we both were caught."

"I wanted to give it to you earlier, but could not find the perfect moment."

"Well, this is the perfect moment, just you and me. The perfect wedding gift." He took her hands in his, reached over the table and kissed her more intimately than before, her lips parting slightly for the second time.

"Well, Mrs. Trout let's enjoy our meal and get going. I don't want to struggle in the dark to find our cabin village." She smiled sweetly at him and took a sip of her coffee, thinking, *you are the perfect Trout. I managed to catch the bigger fish.*